Yellow Chrysanthemum

Short Story Collection

Munmun Samanta "Sam"

Author's Note

"Yellow Chrysanthemum" is a collection of twenty stories, framing twenty women from different strata of society within a single frame. They are different but they are aligned in their roles as oppressed in this patriarchal society.

The title, "Yellow Chrysanthemum," carries poignant symbolism that resonates deeply with the anthology's overarching theme. While this vibrant bloom represents joy and optimism in certain cultural contexts, I have intentionally embraced an alternative interpretation that unfurls the essence of the stories within.

Here, 'Yellow Chrysanthemum' represents the neglected love and unwavering endurance that these women embody. It is a powerful metaphor for their resilience in the face of adversity, and their ability to persist and bloom even in the most challenging circumstances.

These twenty tales, witness the triumphs and tribulations of women who have defied societal constraints, navigating the complexities of their existence with grace and fortitude.

Each story is a testament to the inextinguishable flame that burns within the hearts of those who dare to challenge the status quo, illuminating the path towards a more equitable world for both men and women.

"Yellow Chrysanthemum" is not merely a collection of stories; it is a clarion call to acknowledge the strength and resilience within every woman, a celebration of their ability to overcome and transcend the boundaries imposed upon them by a gender-biased society.

Munmun Samanta "Sam"

Contents

Caged Bird Sings Another Song

Don't spread your wings so high
they will be clipped, and you will die
falling headlong,
thrashing on the ground
slipping down the mound of your
audacity.
Keep in mind,
you are just a woman, after all.

They like to see you caged,
constricted in social pledge,
humble, docile, and camouflaged,
under their glory.

Do not you know?
A caged bird never sings her own song.
She is just allowed,
to rejoice at others, not at her own.

They will be everywhere, always,
to harness your gear,
to shout the harangue of their jeers,
strangulating your cheers.

Don't soar so high.
How dare you touch the sky?

Your wings are made of wax.

They will melt when unfurled,
to reach the sun, the emancipation.
The blood is caked and scabbed
at your every footstep
that defies the iron cage of social
manacles.

Just keep in mind that ensuing future,
You may be cut down and butchered
for their feast of chauvinism.

But be brave to kindle your flame
But be bold to shake off the shame
entitled on you.
spreading out the plumage under your
shining resplendence.

Foreword

Munmun Samanta, "Sam," and I met more than eight years ago. We were co-editors of a global literary publication. She was, and is, an accomplished crafter of magical memorable short stories.

It is an honor and a privilege to introduce you to these women of India, in this, illuminating and insightful, collection.

"Yellow Chrysanthemum" is an ode to the diverse women of India. You will meet them in the houses where they dwell. Each woman Is an uncelebrated hero.

In this patriarchal society, women come in third, the husband reigns. He is the undisputed king of his castle. The children, rears without any assistance, are second. Male children are valued from birth.

Though she serves her husband, in an arranged marriage, as a dutiful daughter-in-law to his aged parents, affectionate mother and grandmother, always available bed-companion, imaginative chef, and frugal housekeeper, she toils tirelessly, year after year without praise or gratitude.

"Sam" writes about each woman's life in stories that illustrate their struggles. We learn about their lives from interior monologues, which are as raw as they are intimate.

In "The Shut Door," Sitesh's wife learns of her unfaithful husband's death, not from grieving children or in-common friends, but from a letter in the regular post that takes seven days to reach her!

In "The Dawn of Sia's Dream," we learn of a mindset that prevails to this day. "Women only write grocery lists and check children's homework." Sia yearns to be a writer.

In "A Home of One's Own," we meet Shekhar's wife. Her greatest wish is to carve out a place for herself where she can enjoy personal writing projects, eat what she wishes whenever she chooses. This woman is willing to do just about anything to accomplish the goal of her own home.

Each of the women are strong-willed. They may keep their dreams to themselves, but they have not abandoned them. Despite the negativity that surrounds them, the absence of female friends, as pillars of loving support, and emotional a distance within their empty marriages, they still cling to dreams. They do not bury hopes so deep that they cannot connect with them. On the surface, they are easy to dismiss. There exists a pervasive sadness, but each woman has something of value within her. It could be "a special dish," a curry that she is proud of and shares with a woman she has never met. Shekar's wife speaks for all the women when she writes these words.

"I am going to make my home, my identity, my life. I am going to find my address."

Each one is trapped, caged. Sometimes it is a gilded cage. Sometimes their abode is a paltry shack. They share an unvoiced dream to escape their cage. Freedom is each woman's fervent desire. That dream is where their individual power lives. It fuels their souls and becomes the means for their escape.

Welcome to the journey of "Yellow Chrysanthemum." Sam's heroes will stay with you long after you turn the last page.

Jill Sharon Kimmelman
American Poet
Winter 2025

Mother India

The cloud is busy locking up the moon when Fatema reaches the bus stop. Her breath wheezes, struggling for air as she walks hurriedly while carrying the toddler and the load. In her shrunken bosom, the child is whining in an accusing monotone. She scurries the way from the Station Goods Store to the Toll Gate to catch up with others, but her fatigued legs betray the speed. The last bus has gone loading all of them, leaving Fatema and her children huffing against the dissolving sunrays. She frantically glances from side to side as she wipes her sweaty forehead with the dirty fringe of her saree. The other two, already drooped in hunger and heavy toil, have crumpled on the ground near the roadside Tamarind tree, covered in dirt and red splotches. The old, patched sacks weighed with grains, mud, and filth feel heavier on her tired shoulders and hands. Fatema feels helpless as she watches the afternoon marching towards the musty darkness with the occasional flicker of lightning in the sky.

With the first crow cawing, she wakes up and taking the children in her firm grip runs for the bus, tramping the fresh dew drops on the sleepy grasses in the courtyard. Reaching the Patakala Toll Gate, they take the narrow muddy road through the bank of Darakeshwar to the Rail Station. They must reach the wagon store before the goods train arrives.

There are Sabina, Mitali, Jarina and others. The vision of fresh rice, and wheat, dripping and scattering all over accelerates their bare feet on the stony red soiled road. They gather and scramble when the laborers carry the heavy grain sacks on their backs. A handful of grains fall like a fountain of gold and silver from the rips of tattered gunny. Like frantic wild animals, they clutter on the dust with crawling knees under the unforgiving sun. Scratching the ground with nails they pick up the grains, which are most precious. In their bruised fists they scoop rice mixed with dirt and fill their sacks. Their faces sweaty and pungent glitter with determination. They do not care about the greasy stick of the police, the abusive red eyes of the supervisors, and the vulgar words of the coolies. No feelings of embarrassment, fear, pain, or hatred can subdue them. The hunger flaming in their bellies is far more substantial than anything else.

Fatema felt hesitant and nervous at the beginning. But cruel poverty and the starved faces of the children compelled her to agree.

Jamal Sekh, Fatema's father chose Sadik, the strong, chestnut-colored man as her husband. He had valid hope for his daughter's happiness as Sadik was diligent and young. He was a peddler, selling cheap plastic cups, glasses, buckets, and other household things through the distant remote villages of Taldangra, Bibarda, and Simlapal on his cycle. On the way back home in the evening, he used to deliver scrap iron to the Mahajan at Vadul More for extra money. Life was hard but it was possible to manage somehow. In the meantime, Fatema became a mother of two girls. Her body sagged under the strain of hardship and childbearing. She could sense Sadik's attention drifting away from her. Finally, the tenuous bonding ripped with the birth of their third daughter. Sadik no longer cared for her. Mehedi, the neighbor's daughter, with all the youthful vitality, attracted Sadik and he eloped with her.

Rumors spread that they had settled near Jamjuri. Fatema called the Moulabi, the Village Chief, but got no justice. She cried, accused, and got ill but nothing came out of it. She had no will to live but looking at the children, the instinct of a mother to sustain her babies stirred within her. She had to feed them. But how? When one day Jarina said, "Let's go to the wagon store of Bankura Station with us. You and your children can collect grains. How long will you and your children starve?" Fatema agreed. There was no way out of it. Her father was no longer alive, and her brothers were poor; they had their own families to feed. From that day Fatema started her new struggle.

With the others, she boards the first bus wrapping the toddler in her lap tightly with the ragged saree and holding the two others in her hands. The conductor behaves miserly with her as she cannot give fare for the children. The bus does not want to take them; they are just burdens, with no profit, only loss. Other passengers also cringe on their faces and look with disdain. Fatema ignores their oozing contempt, the conductor's uneasiness. They should not bother about these trifling humiliations of life. Life is much more precarious for them.

But what should Fatema do today? The sky is already cloudy, and it is a long distance. They must return to their village anyhow. The children are tired. A truck horrendously halts at the Toll Gate. A grizzled traffic police stretches his right palm at the driver through the window. His betel leaf-stained teeth look vulgar under the dim streetlight. Fatema advances towards the driver and with tears in her eyes pleads, "Babu please take us, there is no bus, and the children are dying of hunger and fatigue, please Babu take us. Allah Kasam, I am in great danger."

The truck driver eyes Fatema for a moment and then speeds up with a clamor of the engine blowing stifling black smoke over the hapless face of Fatema. She repeats the same prayer to every vehicle, but no one pays heed to her. She implores the passers-by for help but under their cold indifferent eyes, she only cringes within. Seeing the children, already lying under the roadside tree, tears gush out of her eyes flooding her sunken cheeks and cracked lips. The children need food, they have not eaten anything since the morning.

When they get home Fatema can wash the grains well and boil them with a dry chili and salt. But what can she do now? She feels the coins tied at the end of her saree's knot, but she needs to save them for the bus fare.

Night descends on the toll gate. The curved sickle of the waning moon is nowhere to be seen. An owl screeches from her hidden abode of the tamarind tree. Being tired, Fatema slumps on the road in abysmal confusion. Her back aches from the strain of carrying the baby and the heavy load. Her pale appearance shivers in fear and apprehension. Suddenly she rises from her stupor and wakes the sleepy cubs, "Let us walk to the Dhaldangar More, where the road splits into three paths. There we will flag down the cars or stand in front of them until any of them pick us up. Can't you? We can reach within half an hour if you speed up."

Fatema lifts the toddler in her left lap. Then balancing one sack on the head and the other on her right hand, starts walking. Four small lanky feet shuffle at her back. Dark clouds unshackle the moon from its grip. It beams on their heads like a halo.

The Special Dish

There was no cafe or restaurant around. When Jaya reached the station, it was already 7.30, and in a suburban area like station,

Mithilaganj, night descended earlier than usual. She could hear the rumbling of her belly, and her train was one hour late. After a few desperate searches, she finally decided to have her dinner at a grimly faced red-eyed counter where the dozing face was dashing his forehead on the desk continually and then getting erected in a reflex. He was chanting a mantra repetitively though slurred due to his sleepy tongue, "Come, come, hot rice and veg curry, special dish."

Two or three men were sitting on the unsteady benches, and a woman was sitting next to them on a chair. She looked tired but her eyes sparkled when she turned and found Jaya. She nudged the man on the counter and mopping her stained hand at the fringe of the saree came forward to welcome her.

"Come Didi (sister), I am going to put the pot out from the oven. It's hot with warm smoke, take your seat."

"And what is your special dish?" She asked. The urgency and hope in her voice was palpable.

Jaya guessed the reason. It was the prospect of that promising 'special dish.' A hotel in this area, though not in tough competition, could not make a remarkable sale with the rice, dal, and curry menu. It left very little profit to count, but for the special dishes, they could earn something from the passengers who incriminated their journey before resuming the next. But why should they halt in this godforsaken land?

There was something special for which people used to come here from far-off places. A lucky charm banyan tree at around 2 km from the station with its myths and stories at every leaf of it, dry or green, boosted the popularity of this otherwise insignificant place. Near an old temple, this tree whose age was quite near 105 years stretched out the innumerable branches to make a canopy of green over the wretched temple top which was as hollow to touch the sky above. The temple walls were tattered from the bulging roots of the tree all around the arena and its crevices were well utilized by numerous small trees as their breeding ground. At every branch, small and big, the greyish-brown skin is decked with zillions of red wish knots, simmering like flying red-colored flags at the north breeze. The big fat trunk smeared with vermillion looked like an obese woman draped in a red saree. At the bottom, idols of many sizes and materials were huddled in their dominance in healthy competition. An idol of Lord Shiva was left there for the devotees. It had no fear of being washed away in huge raindrops filtering through the generous umbrella of the big benign banyan tree.

Jaya approached the woman, who looked at her in anticipation. There was something in her look that captivated her, a sense of homeliness. Did she know her? But she never stepped here before. She just came for the first time to add all the details of the miracle tree and the old temple to her thesis paper. She had to submit her final copy the next year and she was in a hurry not to miss any vital spot. Already she had poked into forty-three ancient temples of historical importance in the county. She chose to research the history of the ancient temples. But what about the people? The people, sharing the same soil as the magic tree and temple, did not deserve the same attention. History cannot be the accumulation of mere facts and facades. History always follows its inhabitants.

"Let's sit first," Jaya smiled at her.

 The woman took Jaya to the center table and mopped it repeatedly as if to erase the old stubborn stench mark from it. Then she called the lanky boy and ordered him to serve the food. She did not wish to leave her alone as if she might run away ignoring the lure of the special dish. So, riveting her through her fixed gaze, she smiled nervously.

And when the plate arrived, she looked at Jaya and asked again,

"What will be the special dish, didi?"

It seemed that in her answer lay the best deal of the day. Jaya smiled sheepishly and with a guilt-ridden soul said, "I prefer eating simple at night, otherwise I feel sick."

"But the food is homely. The chicken is our own."

Jaya asked her to sit beside her.

"Sister, I have wandered through your village the entire day, I've come to meet your mystery tree and the temple and now I have to go back. I'm tired and any rich food would be bad for my digestion at this hour. Sorry, dear."

There was something in Jaya's voice that she seemed to accept. Smiling she sat in front of her, keeping her chubby face on the rack of two adjoining palms.

Jaya took her first morsel, and the aroma of local spice heaved her appetite. She asked the woman, "Who made the curry?"

"I made the curry. Isn't it delicious?"

"Yes, it is."

"You know it is quite simple, and I learned this from my grandma."

Thus, the flow of conversation started. As Jaya was taking her slow morsels, the other woman went on chatting to her heart's content. The two men went away paying for their meals and the boy started his scrubbing and washing for the night. His eyes were red in over-exertion.

The man, dozing on the counter, rose and stumbled against the corner of the table.

"Hey, have you dipped your eyes in booze?" The woman sneered at him as he pushed himself up from the seat with a significant effort and headed towards the back of the inn.

The woman looked at him, ignored his existence with the back of her hand, and joined Jaya.

"Then, how many children have you?"

"None." Jaya replied most cordially.

"I also have none."

From the subdued cheer in her voice, it was evident that Jaya had given her some relief from the feelings of jealousy and unhappiness in competition with a woman though the red threads that flag on the trunk of the magic banyan tree kept her prayer also.

"Oh! What have not I done, all the rituals, penitence, whatever they advised for a baby, a baby of my own? But nothing worked, you know." She said amiably.

"Is that your husband?" Jaya asked just to be sure.

"Who? That pot-bellied? Oh no, he is my partner. We are in business, fifty-fifty. You know." She giggled with faint pride making her Betel leaf-stained lips juicier.

"I have a husband though, but you know," she hushed at Jaya's ear, "He has fled with a girl of half his age. I haven't told anyone, such a shame." Then with some hesitation, she added, "But words fly behind your imagination. All knew the fact; I realized when they looked at me with pity." She added, "I don't like pity in their eyes. Who cares? If he could not hold his dignity, who am I to blame? My fate? No, never. Not even that dung-dried bitch."

Jaya looked at her. She had already finished her meal and was waiting for her to end the story. But she was not in any mood to stop.

"Where is your husband?" the woman asked eagerly. "I also have one but now I'm a divorcee," Jaya shrugged.

"Why?"

"I cannot keep track of his socks."

Her gaping mouth and the fallen face made it clear that she could not understand what Jaya just let out. It was not so simple though. Jaya sighed and tried to explain.

"You know I am a student of history. I'm good at keeping the names of kings and queens in perfect order and their dozens of offspring, but not efficient in keeping the computation of my husband's socks, handkerchiefs, and underwear as well as his whimsical moods. I would never be able to project those things to him at his right hand at the right time. So, I failed as a bride."

"Oh, I see," she drawled with her big 'O' shape, parting her lips as if to kiss someone but frozen in a statue.

Jaya took the fun of her way of apprehension and waited patiently for the next question. Usually, she did not like this type of conversation and never allowed any poky nose in her personal life. But in a solitary station area, at a lonely semi-rural hotel with a rustic woman with no pretense, no vanity she felt almost at ease after long years.

Her next question was what did Jaya do to earn money?

"Umm, I am teaching at a school and also trying to learn something more in my extra time." Jaya tried to make her understand simply. And she was quick-witted.

"It's good. I also passed my 10th class after that lecher fled. And the village Panchayat has a post for me. I will do that if I get it, but I also like to work here with my special dishes."

Jaya looked at her watch. "Now I should leave unless my train will leave me here with you."

"It will be fine then." She smiled genuinely.

Jaya rose and washed her mouth.

She opened her bag and asked for the cost of the plate.

"It is just 30 but if you take that special dish then it would have been 100 or 150 as per the number of pieces."

From her tone her grief for that expected money was apparent. Jaya chuckled.

She took a two hundred rupee note and put it on her palm.

"Have you not any change? The pot belly has gone and the key to the cashbox is with him. I've no money to give you back."

"I need no change. It's all yours."

She flung back,

"Oh, I cannot take this unless you take my special dish."

Jaya smiled at her and took her hand into her.

"Who says you have not served your special dish to me? Your hospitality and kindness were something so special that I will never forget in my life. Give the thirty rupees to your partner and keep the rest with you. You must buy something for yourself from it and it will remind you of a woman who visited your village and who could not-"

Jaya struggled to find the right word,

"Who could not keep count of her husband's socks," the woman completed the words for her.

Both burst into laughter, tearing the veil of silent night. When the ripples of their laughter subsided the faint sound of railway announcement reached their ears. Jaya squeezed her hand and stepped into the dark road following the station light. She had to travel back to her world.

Peacock's Feather

I found the peacock's feather on page fifteen of my history book. It looked nice, and vibrant  upon the rusty crown of old Shah Jahan (1628-1658), the great Mughal Emperor. Nikhil gave it to me and told me to keep consistent vigilance over it.

"It has a miracle power," he says, "It will grow and even give you one or two more out of it." I should not believe him but there was nothing in my adolescent heart except an unperturbed dedication to him. So, I did that every day. Sometimes three or four times a day, I used to watch the feather if it was growing or giving birth to a new one. I did this till I was promoted to a new class. Then I lost it in the smell of new books. It also failed to show any miracle till then, a whole academic year.

Time flowed like a river but not in a meandering way. It was steadfast and adamant in its punctuation and determination, keeping pace with the hour, minute, and second, diligently. I grew older and my head started collecting more air in its vacuum than a mere peacock's feather. In the place of one feather, I dipped my brain in thousands of peacock feathers to be grown and reproduced with multiple iridescences. But nothing worked. Page fifteen of Geometry, Nesfield's English Grammar, and page forty of Hazlitt, History of Britain, Saussure, and Structuralism, even in Virginia Woolf there were they, either blue, yellow, scarlet, or green. But dashing all my hope, no one fed my fancy. Life hit hard. Embarrassment, the counterpart of defeat, was enough to strangulate my fantasy. I no longer wait for them to grow or reproduce a new one. I let them vanish. There was no dawdle time left in my mature dawn for any magic.

Then one day after ten long summers, I met him again. He said, "He had waited for me." I felt baffled and trapped. I wished to return all the colored feathers and to tell him to go away. I did not want them anymore. I did not want him anymore. But I could not find any of them. So, I bowed my hand and tolerated all his gibberish till I had mustered the courage to say 'no' to him before walking away.

I did not believe in such trash, no more. Many a time I had made myself a clown. My life had been shattered by these fanciful thoughts, and I no longer believed in such nonsense.

My life had been devastated due to those fanciful thoughts that I carried in my head, and I no longer believed in any nonsense. My husband had left me for another woman and now I wished not to search those peacock feathers and let another man enter my life. I told him I hated pity as much as I hated him. I sacked him out of my door and shut it tightly.

 I also closed the door tightly on my mind, leaving no room for whimsical ideas to encroach. I needed hard, demanding work to keep my thoughts occupied.

I started dusting my bookshelf. I must discard some old stuff to give sufficient space for new ones. Suddenly, something touched my finger as I flipped the pages searching for a truant cockroach. It was so soft and light, like a piece of old cotton or the love of my grandmother.

There it was on page 35 of the tricolored flag of India. I had misplaced it many years ago. I wanted to run to him, shouting his name. I wish to say sorry. But I felt I had misplaced my love many years ago and could not place it again in my crippled heart, not anymore.

The Caged Bird

The black pupils on the orange iris, frightened and desperate, fighting for freedom. Sometimes it tries to tear the iron bars with its crooked beak in utter desperation, sometimes it screams in extreme bafflement, to grasp the current situation in which it is forced to live, differentiating it from the previous.

Kamal brought it yesterday.

"Poor pitiful creature, ah ha. My little parakeet, my captive sojourner." She caresses its neck as she puts the 'chana' bowl inside. "You are my chic; you are my nestling." She makes a sound of sympathy as she feels sorry for it or pleased, secretly. She at least can move, can unburden her bereaved heart somewhere in the attic or the dense thick sugarcane field in the absence of Kamal. But it cannot. The half-round cage is its only world now. How poor!

Earlier, she used to visit the fields, letting her knee-length dark hair free upon her solid back and billowy bosom. The morning breeze caressing the ripe crops used to touch her and whisper as she giggled. The fresh, slightly damp air, infused with the fragrance of Gulancho—a flower with white petals gathered around a yellow center—played in her wavy tresses.

That was the story of bygone days.

"Why do you let your hair open outside? You shameless minx."

"I like the zephyr, blowing on my face," she used to murmur shyly.

"I will show you how to like it." The gnawed answer and clattering teeth made the new bride shiver. That evening Kamal cut her hair with his honed sickle ignoring her heart-wrenching cry and pleading.

Kamal is her husband, 10 years older. He is robust and virile in front of her dainty posture. He never makes love to her, just punishes her with the excuse of any mistake, trivial or serious. Maybe this is his way of gratification. Tihar also could not love him, though she tried when she came into this house as a new bride with a big round nose ring and red saree. She had exercised all her inherent womanly skills to develop so-called 'feelings' within his monstrous heart. But his solid sulky furrow and loveless core dissolved all her futile attempts. She just coiled in front of that stone-framed face where not a single line was tender in emotion.

Now she lives in this house under Kamal's vigilance- cooks food, cleans households, helps him in the field, takes care of two children, and remains dutiful in bed. All her maiden dreams for a husband, children, and own home mocks her now. She feels suffocated within the four walls of her life - The Cage.

Nitesh, Kamal's closest friend, would occasionally visit in the evenings when Kamal returned from the fields. They would chat until the children fell asleep on the floor near the smoldering fire. Kamal lay motionless on the ground, half-drunk and half-asleep. She quietly unlatched the door, waiting for Nitesh to leave. When she came back, her cheek turned red as she sluggishly rubbed the spot where Nitesh had kissed her before leaving.

She peeped furtively at the mercury-stained mirror on the wall and smiled as she arranged the bed for the children. Her eyes sparkled in a zing, a new note that she could transmit in her own words. Kamal never suspected Nitesh or did not want to. Nitesh was the son of 'Mahajan'(moneylender), and Kamal had to borrow money from him in time of cultivation. So, Nitesh could come into this house at any time with any excuse. But Kamal's torture of little Tihar grew more violent day after day.

But when Nitesh did not come for two or three days she got irritated, bitter, and afraid. She could not concentrate on anything. "You bitch, where is your mind"? Kamal hissed in bed as he forced himself on her. Tihar cried out in pain and humiliation and out of her grief for Nitesh's unknown absence.

Kamal has gone to work. Tihar gives the bird red chili and 'chana' and tries to teach it something good to say. But it is so stubborn to utter any single voice except a cracking protest. Kamal returns from the field quite early and is in a festive mood. He changes himself into his best attire and asks Tihar for his torch. She does not ask him anything. She is already in a bad mood for Nitesh and does not want to be snapped at again.

But Kamal speaks out: "Shut the door properly. I will be late at night."

Tihar cannot control it anymore:

"Why? Where will you go?"

"Nitesh had married. Today is the feast. He invites all his friends. He also calls for you, but I say you must stay home with the kids."

Kamal goes out leaving a stone statue of Tihar at the doorstep. Children are sleeping, lapping one another. Tihar steps into the premises, framed against the sky by the hanging full moon. Everything is imperturbably calm in this brimming moonlight. The parakeet is dozing on its perch. Tihar coos and it wakes up with a grunting shriek. Silently she unlocks the door. The bird does not move. Tihar steps back from the open cage door and whispers, "Go away, you petty bird, go away." The bird changes the sitting position on the perch and says "crako crako"

"Fly you duffer, fly." Tihar hisses impatiently, "Have you forgotten the test of freedom in one day?"

But the bird just nods its head to Tihar in an upright attitude and starts to prune the feathers.

Desperately Tihar snatches the bird out of its cage, puts it on the courtyard's edge, and pokes its tail. At first, it looks suspiciously towards Tihar and then steps ahead gingerly. Tihar's face glows in joy as the bird spreads its languid wings and gradually takes motion far above the old margosa tree.

"Eh, goodbye." She keeps looking at the bird until its yellow-green feathers trail away from her sight.

She comes back to her bed and waits for Kamal to return. At first, she shivers at the thought of the consequence of her just finished project but then a profound peace washes over her eclipsing the fear.

The Dawn of Sia's Dream

The dew drops are soft and wet on her skin. Sia shivers as the morning air caresses the bare skin of her neck and shoulder. The light is thrifty now as if a dilemma is still going on the canvas of the sky. Sun rays are peeping to win over the night. But the night is not ready to give up her throne so early. Sia looks anxious. She knows who will win and she must quickly pack her things before the conflict is resolved.

She takes her pen and scribbles on her notebook, lying pensive on her lap. A story is taking shape in her imagination. Threads of varied colors, imbued with emotion, lapped with experience crowd her memory and jostle to get etched in ink. Plots and characters bounce around her entire day screaming for release. Most of the time she loses them in the turbulent wave of daily chores. And in the course of this hope and hopelessness, she can preserve some clues to build a nest in this wee hour.

Endless tasks fall on her regularly to keep her family afloat. Yet, in her freedom she discovers joy. At least she can hold her pen and paper squeezing out her time. All her sweats and struggles salute her at the end of the day when she watches the crescent moon hanging from the bough of the tamarind tree and her heart slips into deep slumber leaving a wispy smile on her lips.

She loves this part of the garden. But more than that she loves this confluence of light and shadow. Amidst her hectic schedule, it is the only time she can call her own. It is the only time when she can cherish her dream. She remembers the movie "Tangled" and the song, "I've Got a Dream." Everyone has a dream. It just needs to be nurtured. Sia wants to be a writer. She carves out moments from her packed routine to work on her dream. And this is the perfect time to invest.

How desperately she wishes the sun to delay its course, how desperately she prays the time to be a bit slow. She has a thousand jobs to do, and a thousand responsibilities to fulfill.

But one responsibility she cannot ignore. It is her responsibility to her dream, the elixir of her happiness.

She believed she had abandoned her dream the day she got married. A good wife only writes grocery lists and checks kid's homework. Six years of marriage filled her life with cooking, washing, taking care of family members, and being the best bed partner. Being the tethered goat of constant humiliation and threats Sia lost all hope in her life. And when she finally got her divorce, it rained for three nights. Even today she can feel that earthy smell permeating over the field. Sitting beside her window, she watched the dollops of water gathering on the gloomy glass pane. She allowed them to camouflage her tears. How much she waited for this rain! She wrote a poem on rain.

In the ruts of her agony, for the first time in her life, she conceived the beeline of happiness. It was a state of ecstasy and inebriation, but the addiction never betrayed her. Words conjured a beautiful world for Sia, erasing all the dirt scabbed on her soul for years. The sun that came out after three days of arrogant downpours was bountiful as if promising enough life in the dark life of Sia.

Sia undusted her pen and paper before being a single mother of a five-year-old child, before being the only earning member of her aged ailing parents, and before being the elder sister of a younger one who was suffering from Steven Johnson syndrome and epilepsy. The clock is striking six. The eastern sky is taking color. Sia will have to wait for another tomorrow. Sia is ready to wait for a thousand tomorrows.

The Scar

Initially, the scar was not so deep. It was light reddish in contrast with light brown skin. When I showed it to Manish, he took a hurried glance and said "Beautiful." His words intrigued me. I thought he didn't notice it. He was so absorbed with his smartphone! He smiled at me as he spoke, but that did not soothe me. I was sure he was smiling at something else, maybe a text message or an image of someone else whom I didn't know. A scar is not something to smile about but rather a mark that evokes concern. And a scar cannot be 'beautiful.'

The word lingered in my mind giving a lot of digression in my arranged thoughts. I couldn't complete any of my assignments that day. Why did he say 'beautiful'? His voice was indifferent, a lightness in his attitude towards me, that stung me.

Later I decided to raise the matter at night in bed. I would say something sweet and let him kiss my scar. So, I wore a very short sleeve and kept my duvet under my breast with my hands crisscrossed. But he was busy with his laptop. Day by day his work pressure is increasing.

That night I could not sleep well. I could not remember the last night when I slept like a tired child in his embrace. An occasional beep on his mobile and the flicker of light, piercing faintly from the cover of his blanket disturbed my slumber. The burning sensation was increasing somewhere. I was not sure if it was on my hand or in my eyes, deterring pain from liquefying in teardrops.

The next day the scar took a deep scarlet tint. I looked at my hand for some time with disbelief and wondered if it belonged to me or not.

I served Manish breakfast. He did not notice my hand. How could he overlook such a change on my arm? I pondered the entire day till Manish came back home in the evening-tired, drained, and lost.

I made him a hot cappuccino and held my hand before him for a long time, quite unnatural for me. But his eyes were hooked on the TV screen. He was gobbling the sounds and movements of the other world. The thin layer of milk was making a funny mark on his upper lip.

That night I did not sleep. Without waiting for Manish's mobile to wake me up I kept my laptop on. I completed my pending jobs and posted my articles. When I went to sleep late at night, I could hear birds chirping behind my window screen.

The next day when I woke up, Manish was not there beside me. He had gone. Had he eaten his breakfast? Then my thoughts shifted from Manish, and I looked at my scar. It seemed a bit pale. I felt happy for myself. It was healing at last. Grabbing a big cup of coffee, I reclined on the terrace wall and flipped on my laptop. Four of my ten posts were approved, and I was going to be paid within twenty-four hours. I calculated the money and gave a happy cry. I bathed for a long time and dressed in my best attire. I needed to go to the city library to collect some notes for my upcoming projects. When I came out of the library, the noon crawled into twilight. The sky looked mesmerizing. I hurried home. I felt a new spur in my life, something special for me, something to build for myself. Oh! I had forgotten totally. I looked at the scar. Finally, it was gone.

A Home of One's Own

"**Home** is a name, a word, it is a strong one; stronger than a magician ever spoke, or spirit answered to, in the strongest conjuration."

—Charles Dickens

Dear Shekhar,

I can imagine your astonishment when you read this letter. I am thankful to you for allowing me to stay in your house for so long and I hope you will be grateful to me too as I have toiled in your house without any remuneration.

When you get this letter, I will be far off. In this world of smart communication, people cannot get lost except being killed. But I know there will be a thousand reasons for you not to call me back. You know how stubborn I am and how tenacious I can be at a certain point, especially when I'm fighting for what's right for me.

Since my childhood, I have desperately searched for a home. In my father's home, my stepmother's stern gaze never allowed any room for my childhood whims. Every minor transgression was met with a swift, unforgiving 'No.' I was alone and segregated, with no room to cry.

When my aunt invited me to her new house, I felt incredibly happy to join my only cousin. We were of the same age, only a month's gap. My uncle was dead at a very early age. My cousin lost her father as I lost my mother. Most of the time I used to speak with my aunt and my cousin. So, they were not mine. When I entered their new home, my heart leaped in great joy. I had my new home. But one day as I was about to clean some of the stuff like old newspapers and magazines, my aunt said quite sternly, "No need to do this. Tania will be angry if you misplace her things. We will arrange them later. You should enjoy the days you are here." For the first time, I realized I was not included in that circle of "we". I was an outsider, a guest for some days. From my childhood, we were treated as two sisters and my aunt always took the place of my dead mother with her love and care. But years passed before I realized the harsh truth of this world. People say many things, but things are different.

When I grew up and visited my brother's house, my sister-in-law never allowed me in the kitchen. She said I should show my culinary skills in my house. She preferred to keep her house in her way. She was a selfish and harsh woman. That was not the matter. But she just poked the truth with brazen reality. That's all. When a girl is married, she loses her home. A girl has no home of her own.

Even when I became adult enough to take on all the responsibilities of my family, whenever I tried to give my opinion regarding household matters, my father used to tell me not to bother. My brother had all the priorities of finalizing family matters though the responsibilities were on me. It is our general patriarchal chauvinism. But it reminded me that I have no home of my own.

Then I got married and came to your house. My parents said a girl's real address was her in-law's house after marriage. When you told me, "This is my house and if you do not behave accordingly, you can leave it," I did not argue. I came to your house 20 years ago and within these 20 years, you and your parents have told me these words two hundred thousand times. But whenever I wanted to visit my parents you all stopped me saying, "After marriage, this is your house. You cannot go to your parents now and then." I was quite confused. Now I realized that it was a part of the patriarchal game.

If this was not my house, I could have asked you why I was toiling here for twenty long years, giving birth to two sons, taking care of every household matter, and serving minute household needs. Why?

Shekhar, I had so many questions to ask you that I never asked. I always tried to keep the peace of the family, butchering my peace. But silence cannot solve everything. The cacophony of the unresolved questions tortures me to death.

But now I do not want any peace. I think I have not asked you these questions out of any fear of dispute. I did not ask you these questions because I realized you had no answer. I am not going to ask you the questions whose answers you will give through your muscles. I am not afraid of your muscles. But I hate looking at you who is nothing but a duffer. You cannot stand before my reason and just act as a chauvinistic guard. You are a puppet of this society feeding upon the patriarchal potion and serving the pre-destined male role bargaining your reason. This society has offered you huge scope, an enormous opportunity and it has crippled you to your brain. You cannot get out of this comfort zone.

I have done my wifely duties for you. Our sons are grown and settled. I've fulfilled my duties as a mother. Now it's time for me to reclaim my own life.

We are all in search of our roots. Roots give us strength; roots give us sustenance and engraft within us a sense of belongingness. Wherever we travel, wherever we settle, wherever we are forced or entitled to live, we seek our roots, our identity.

You cannot call me back, Shekhar. You cannot bring me to heel with your muscles or your threats. I am not afraid of you anymore. What you always did was nothing but brazen out at my reasoning. I only pity you, for you've chosen to remain a fool, a chauvinist guard serving a system that cripples us all.

I am going to make my home, my identity, my life. I am going to find my address.

A Girl Made of Darkness

"**Everything** is ok, except the color. She is too dark. Even our son is stark fair in comparison."

"Her face is sweet, and her height is tolerable. But she is a Black person in looks. She will only give birth to tars."

"Mira is a talented girl. But we cannot approve the match. Our son is not willing to marry so black a girl. We are so sorry for her."

Pity is another ruse to hurt one's dignity and self-esteem, adding some piquancy to the sadist joy that they want to relish, hurting someone. The innocuous words are so naked in mockery and contempt that they are enough to hack a human heart or paralyze it to death.

It is expected. And she doesn't bother anymore. Her lungs have expelled so many sighs in the long run of her life and her soul tolerates so many virulent scourges. The familiar frisson of being hurt has evaporated from her doe eyes. She lost track of her dogged determination to touch the sky. Yet, sometimes, something hurts. She is not made of ice at last.

She can't say firmly if her mother shrieked out when she first saw her out of her womb and if her father's expectant looks got buried in despair and worries. But she feels the slithering jibes all her life at her back or front. The eyes of pity and disgust she meets at every hive. Her relatives, and friends, all talk about her color; and suggest all the ointments and pastes or home remedies to peel her out of her God-given skin and make her fairer. She cannot discern the real motive of life that she read in books and that society flouts. There is a severe dichotomy between them.

In her early days, her ingenuous eyes could not discern the fault in her, but she was sure that her presence sensitized people's consolidated opinions and triggered them to open their stabbing tongues. They just longed to observe her in pain, self-pity, and writhing humiliation. They enjoyed watching her fomenting in the fume of self-destruction, the penalty of her birth, how daring an act she did by taking birth in this color control society and living like a human being not like an animal at the mercy of others' poking sticks. She wished to crawl inside, digging a deep trench to hide and bury her face, in shame and disgust that the world was pouring on her.

At school, all their friends laughed at her. Their astonished eyes and grisly comments caught the humor so early that she felt she should not come to school anymore. But she learned to fight. "It is not the color but the spirit inside you is the most important power", her parents told her. But at night sometimes she heard the whisper, the suppressed wailing, "If she was a bit fair or if she was a boy"- an unattainable wish. They will never exonerate her from the blame of being dark. Her sleepy nights eluded in the wistful dream, the magical expectation of some miracle that could change her world and the surroundings from black to fair.

Nothing happens. It is all about genetics and melanin as the teacher teaches in the class. The measurement of melanin is high, too high for her. No way can it be reverted, no big banner advertisement or fairness cream gimmick.

Gradually her anguish gets shaped as she grows up and her contemplation orchestrates her disturbing thoughts in her colorful world of a brush stroke. She is emblematic of rainbows, all the colors of the universe merged in her, not in white but in black. She is a girl made of darkness.

In her canvas, she creates the eclectic shadow of that genuine color. Her apathy towards this abysmal mental perversion agitates the mean hearts to act more vulnerable, thirstier for her unconscionable heart. Anyhow they want her to shriek out, anyway, they want her to feel inferior.

She draws so beautifully. Finally, they murmur, "She has some magic in her hands and in that brush. Whatever she draws get back to life." Their applause is silent and smothered with their abominable vile and distrust. But she knows in her heart, she can change her world in colors.

It is a deep night. All have gone to sleep. Their lazy snores are piling on their pillows. The sky is in an uproar and furry, ready to fight. The dark girl emerges from her room and stands in front of the darkness. She feels comfortable in her heart as the dark zephyr caresses her dark hair, falling like a fountain or tide. She promises the dark muse or fairy-something she can offer on her bide.

Coming back into the room she shuts all the windows tight and lit the candle of light. In the deep, dense, dark, its wick flickers like the lighthouse. In her black easel, she fixes the dark canvas. She looks like a bride. Blazing flame, like red vermillion, sparkles on her face in glory and pride.

She draws a beautiful Black girl with wings. Her tenacious passion gives her a shape- black lips, black legs, and black arms. Her black hair was embellished with a thousand stars. The black wings are mooring in mist. She unfurls the wings and stretches them afar with the precise strokes of her brush. When she finishes it with the final addition, all her suppressed suffering reincarnates in a phenomenal woman bird. And it gets life. It starts flying high, soaring above all the opprobrium in her dark room illuminating bright in the stretching dark beyond. Her incarnation was completed. She looks back with pride.

Now she is ready to traverse a long way, the world's applause, where she is no longer a victim of derision but the invincible soul of Prometheus.

Beast of Burden

"**Where** is my dress, Durga?"

"Is the Tiffin ready?"

"My handkerchief is not in the pocket of my trousers."

"What do you do the whole day? Cannot even iron a tie evenly?"

"There is so much debris in the bin. The sofa sheet is wrinkled."

"What are you doing hah?"

"I'm bored with the same Tiffin. My table is in astray. You did not lock the roof door properly at night. You should clean the toilet regularly. See how ferocious the fan blades are looking. Cannot you wipe them up?"

These are just part of the extensive list my husband recites now and then. He takes my name so often that, at times, I feel no one could obstruct his path to salvation. After all, my grandmother named me after Goddess Durga, the one with ten hands.

But I am not that Durga who vanquished the demon. I am just an ordinary housewife with only two hands and ten thousand tasks to complete every day—none of which involve slaying any monster.

I only like to ask my husband, "What do you do the whole day?" But I suppress the query. I know it is the most prohibited question for any "good woman" particularly for "good wives."

I want to scream at his elephant ear – "I wake up with the alarm even when sleep keeps my brain dizzy, my limbs pain in strain for daily drudgery, and ask for more rest, more sleep. I get fresh, soak all the clothes that you, my dear hubby, had just taken care to throw on the floor near the machine the previous night. I start cutting vegetables, washing rice, pulse, fish or meat, or anything that is included in your food list. I work like a spring machine hearing nothing, caring nothing for the hunger that irks my stomach." I want to gush out, but words are as numb as me or I lack the vigor to utter them. So, it continues as it is.

In the middle of my cooking, my beloved spouse shrieks out, "Durga where are my sandals?"

His feet are so big in comparison to mine that there is no question that I may have worn them. Whenever he mounts the bed, he just throws them carelessly inside the narrow gap of the divan. And it is my morning routine to rescue them. Bending on my knees, I take the duster's handle and thrust my head in the deep dark of dust to rescue those precious pair while he meditates on the bed with an irritated freaking face yawing and cursing my low efficacy in this expedition.

Something smells bad.

Oh, God! The curry.

I take off the sandals, and in the process, I bump my head painfully.

"Oh! Durga, cannot you work cautiously? What a mess you create in a trifle."

I have no time to hear his unavailing lecture, so I run to the kitchen to find my hard-toiled curry is burning and over-pouring rice gruel disarrays the oven without caring a fig for my partner's next topic of reprimand. I try my best to control the situation with wartime sincerity, but the freaking order panel starts its course again in my bewildered ears.

"Durga, where have you put my towel?"

"You've put it somewhere at night after using it," I shouted from the kitchen wishing not to leave my battleground.

"I always put it in the right place." He grumbled.

But the sound of clashing utensils and cracking of cumin seeds in oil just ignore the whimper.

I prepared his tea, toast, and boiled egg and hurried to the table. He needs a healthy breakfast. After all, he works in an office inside an air-conditioned cubicle.

I put them on the table.

"Your breakfast."

I utter and rush to the kitchen feeling the squalling in my belly and rebellion of my tossing brain. I have been working from dawn on an empty stomach.

But I just ignore it. I have no time for it. I must finish my cooking and prepare his lunchbox proportionately, maintaining a fine balance of carbohydrates, protein, sugar, and saturated fat. Food is to be cooled before putting in an airtight container. Otherwise, the leakage-proof gutter will be damaged and lose its elasticity as well as utility very soon.

Those gutters! How easily they get damaged unlike the women like me who are not allowed to get damaged.

Is it?

I recall my mom. She used to tell me this often when I would fondle my elastic hair band, and she was ready to comb my hair.

"Durga never pulls the elastic too much; it will lose its elasticity and will tear apart. And don't wrench any relation out of its capacity. Anything related to capacity and tolerance will break one day."

I would turn back, finding her forlorn eyes smothering in unknown pain and self-pity.

"What's up, Mom?"

"Nothing." Her tone dropped. I then wished to kiss her pale shrunken cheeks. My mom. My dear mom.

Sometimes I also feel so – on the verge of breaking off my tenacity as if cracking out of a pan, scattering all over, howling, shouting, creating a mess. I feel overwrought. But I swallow my anger, hatred, and humiliation day after day. I have buried my voice in the labyrinth of my meaningless life. I have turned into a beast of burden- all at his disposal, a slave to my husband.

"Durga, what's the hell of you? You keep breakfast open on the table. Just care a fig for health and hygiene. How many times have I to tell you this?"

I say nothing, just twinge like a stricken beast with silent mortification.

I assume he comes to the breakfast table as early as I turn my back to the kitchen what he usually does every day. So, I feel no need to put a lid and even if I do so I must rush back with the sound of pulling a chair to open them off again for him. Otherwise, he will shout "Durga, you know I am going to sit for breakfast, what is the need for putting lids on them? It is only a trick to kill my precious time." Then he will provide a long lecture on the importance of time and how I lack the sense of it. Huh!

I just mute myself and allow him to throw up his grievance, and disgust on me. And then he leaves finishing his breakfast, slamming the polished wooden door behind me.

I hold my breath for a second and blink for some time as if to adjust to the vacuum of sudden freedom as well as silence. Then I clean everything on the table and check the lock carefully repeatedly. Now I wish to be all alone, at least for some time. I dust and wash up the kitchen and rooms before arranging everything in order.

 Then on a plate, I arrange my food and come to the balcony. This is my time, my quality time with me. This time I need to sit and think and chew.

This is my everyday routine. When I was a new bride, I was more energetic and bubbling. I indulged in household chores even out of my capacity to please my husband.

Was I successful? Did he ever feel pleased and blessed? Did he ever utter a kind word to me in place of abuse?

I take a big morsel and peep outside the bars. The streets are now busy handling the hustle and bustle of moving crowds and vehicles. I like to watch these with a languid mood. The clock is turning eleven and after finishing my meal, I must take a bath. But I love to watch the busy city underneath. I look out thrusting my weary face on the bars of the window.

A bulky man with a pot belly is thrashing a van driver who is already struggling to move his van with a huge burden of goods. The skinny, bone-decked, weak man can't paddle the van properly with feeble foot pressure. But the plump man who cannot bear his body weight and cannot move an inch without gasping for air continuously keeps charging the van-man of laziness and condemning him with harsh words. I forget to finish my food. I shove my head closer to the bars, trying to get a clearer look, waiting with bated breath for the catastrophe—what will happen next? I feel terrible. Excitement hammers at my brain, sending shivers through my body. My eyes widen, as if I'm trying to envision my destiny.

Can he bear the load?

Will the paddle move?

Will it...?

Uma

They had gone, one after another. Tridib had gone on the ritual day. He managed a one-day-leave on emergency. His office did not grant leave without any seven days' notice, even when one's father died. Why on this Earth did people die without any intimation? Science is stepping ahead of everything. But no one can envisage death, slowly or abruptly, crawling or slithering, in which way it pounces and seizes its prey. Uma sighed.

Did she foresee that? Everything was usual, perfect, pristine. Vabotosh Mukherjee was not at all a messy person mentally or physically. Everything he did with priggish perfection. He never ran with time, rather, time had to keep pace with him. 5.00 A.M.: waking up, sipping warm water with honey and lemon, going out for a walk, 6.10 A.M.: Coming back to get fresh and have a healthy breakfast at 8.30 with butter, bread, egg, and banana. Everything in his life was disciplined and flawless. His nails to hair, tie to socks, hairbrush to the wristwatch, all were arranged in immaculate perfection. But only one thing was not perfect in his life, his wife Uma.

Uma was not the perfect companion for him. Vabotosh always made her feel imperfect. If a love marriage was possible for him ignoring the glaring eyes of guardians, he never had married Uma. Uma never cared for perfection. Her hair, like the nimbus cloud, always dangled here and there surrounding her tiny round face. Her nose is flat, and her forehead is broad. Her teeth were all arranged in chaos as if they had forgotten their allocated seats and sat here and there jumbled together. But when she smiled, she looked childish and beautiful. Vabotosh never said that. Her mother used to say. Vabotosh always grumbled and whined at her clumsy ways of being. She used to forget her comb and often placed it on his table. She forgot to close the window when the south wind tormented the glass fineries decked in the closet. She allowed them to blow, carrying dry leaves, dust, wild petals, and the rare smell of bygone memories. She loved to race with the wind in her little restless heart. She never cared to dress up perfectly when going out. For her simplicity was beauty and for him arduous perfection. She was so shameless to sing loudly now and then beside the window at night or whenever she wished to. She used to giggle even at the trivial jokes of the servants or vegetable man. He had to check all those uncivilized habits of hers with his uncivilized crackdowns. Yes, she became silent to some extent but only in his presence and this enraged Vabotosh too much. Often, he found her singing on the roof in a low voice chattering gleefully with the neighbor or sipping tea together with the maid. She had no dignity.

Uma never cared how much Vabotosh detested her till one day he declared she should change her room as he could no longer tolerate the burden of sharing the bed with an unmannered woman. Though at first, she took it as a new prank, later she realized how serious he was. She realized even after 10 years of their marriage how annoying and unwanted she was to him. How pathetically he had to tolerate her, though she gave birth to his four children.

Now they had gone, Atashi, Manasi, Sudip, and Tridib- one after another. Manasi's eldest son is preparing for the final exam of class ten and Sudip joined a new job. Atasi's mother-in-law is ill. Everyone has his or her own life.

She is alone. In slow steps, she enters Vabotosh's room. A picture is hanging over the bed on the wall, a well-groomed smug face decked with fresh garland.

His smile was perfect. As Uma scrutinized the picture she thought. He smiled cautiously as if keeping in mind how many teeth he would show and how to sidetrack the rest without bulging his cheeks. His mustache is perfectly pruned and colored. Uma looked at his eyes, her heart shivered, they were like the eyes of a living man. She felt as if he was inspecting her even from that dead world, scanning all her manners. Unconsciously she arranges the pleats of her saree, looks at her bangles, and checks his table again to see if she has forgotten her comb there. Uma locks the room and stows the key in the cupboard. Malati, the cook, has taken leave for two days after these 15 days of drudgery, and chaos. It is fine. She can manage on her own.

An overpowering silence descends upon the house. The children are no longer shouting, the cooks are no longer scrambling their utensils. Consistent calling, shouting, talking, whispering, yelling, and gossiping all have stopped slowly as if a tornado has gradually dwindled to perfect quietude.

Uma feels this calmness as soothing as well as disturbing. Sudden freedom is unleashed on her as she feels aimless about what to do, where to start, and what next.

The daughters, sons, and daughters-in-law were pleading with her to go with them.

"What will you do in this forlorn house? Come with us. Stay with us."

"I'll go, but not now. Let me stay for some days and arrange things."

Uma knows they will gradually forget to ask, and she would be happy enough to live on her own.

Uma started wandering through the rooms, kitchen, dining, study, guest room, and garage, and finally, she halted in her room. A flush of satisfaction washes over her. She opens the windows and lets the breeze blow freely, excluding all the norms and boundaries. She looks at her messy corners and cuddles in the bed. She finds perfect peace. She has not to be startled by a mere sound of accusation. She does not have to attend to anyone or anything against her will. She feels free and light like a feather ready to waft in the morning breeze.

She inhales the air, there is Tridib's smell, Manasi's, Atashi's, Sudip's smell- the smell of childhood, the smell of pranks, the smell of anger, tears, smiles, giggles, the smell of care and affection, the smell of abhorrence and abomination.

There are a lot of things she must detangle now, the death and afterward. Vabotosh had died suddenly. These days she doesn't have time to think about it. Everything happened so quickly. Now she has enough time to ruminate. She tries to recall everything from scratch.

What happened that day? Uma left her bed and found he had not gone to walk. The main gate was locked as she had bolted it last night.

"What was wrong with him? "

Uma thought as she entered his room. The curtains were drawn closely and not a single window was opened. Over the head, the fan was whirling at the fullest spade. The morning sun was burgling into the room ignoring the red eyes of the blinds. In that dim light, Uma discovered him lying on the bed, perfectly still. His room was in perfect order, but something was wrong with him. A pristine white blanket was drawn to his chest. As Uma touched him the frigid coldness sipped through her spine, and she shrieked out in horror and disbelief.

She didn't cry. She took time to understand death, so close and so near yet she could not presage any signs or symptoms on him the previous night. He was dead, dead, and cold.

She touched him, on his hand, stiff and still. Then she checked the heartbeat. No sound of life was there. She dialed the numbers one after another. Children, relatives, people broke out with sympathy, love, care, and affection.

"Don't cry, don't cry" don't break down," they showered soothing words. It was so confusing for her to correctly construe her emotions. So many knots were coiling inside me, so many hues of sentiments were bubbling that I was not sure which one to give preference. Should she cry? Should she remain calm and mute? What would be her right expression before this spectacular world? She felt confused and guilty. People cry over their losses. When Vabotosh died, she could not manage to decide what she had lost. What was Vabotosh to her? Husband or Master? Of course, she got two boys and two girls out of their marriage knot. But it was not everything. Was there any trace of respect, love, or affection between them?

The children are married and settled. What life she spent as his wife, caretaker, and housekeeper appears too insignificant to her. She provided him with food and necessary things from time to time. She dared not to sing loudly, go out, speak, or laugh. She had so many faults, so many blemishes! She might have disfigured his image.

She feared to unfurl herself. He was always there to find fault with her, to judge her, to criticize her, to taunt her, to dehumanize her.

Why should she cry?

From the bed, she looks out the window. The garden is blooming with white beauty under the bewitching moonlight. When Vabotosh ordered her to choose a room she had chosen this at the farthest corner, far from him adjoining the garden. The room is small and stuffy. But in her imagination sometimes it bellows, till it starts floating. And Uma begins to giggle as if the bloated room is tickling her. Pressing her face on the bed she starts laughing. She cannot control it anymore. Something is twirling inside her and wave after wave of laughter chokes her, drawing tears from her eyes. Being unable to stop it suddenly Uma breaks out into sobbing.

In the garden, an owl startles and flaps its wings in confusion. The aroma of wild

Hasnuhana (the name of a flower) permeates the night sky.

Uma is free now.

Bright Big Bananas

"Anu, Anuu."

When the call reached Anu, she was wrestling with the burble of tap water, scrubbing the utensils.

"What's ma?" Anu yelled back without pausing her tireless hands, busy erasing the stubborn stains under the pan. The housekeeper was absent for two days, and she had to catch the bus to the office. It never waited for her a second. Who stopped for whom? - Philosophy of life. She had already practiced deducing a philosophical conclusion over everything. This added a scoop of metaphysical dessert over her ever-grumbling mundane dishes and assisted her to sinew the weakened muscles of desperation with the sprinkling satisfaction of spasmodic stoicism. Life was such a hard-core pragmatic brut.

It was 7.55.32 A.M. in the kitchen clock, and she would have to rush within ten minutes. She was gasping for breath like a bellow.

"What are you doing? Cannot even finish with the dishes? Oh! In my time I had to swab a thousand utensils within a blink. The relatives used to come and go like a swarm of locusts. One day two of your father's friends came suddenly without any notice."

"And you must cut a big fish on your own as father was not at home. Then you cut your finger, and you must cook even with your bandaged thumb." Anu narrated the last part of the anecdote as she emerged from the kitchen and stood in front of her mother's chair while mopping her hands in a towel. Anu watched her mother. Her face looked visibly irritated at this unwanted disruption. The story she was meant to finish should not be completed by others in certain haste.

"How did you know?" She grumbled.

"Because you told me all these zillion times since I was 9 or 10 and now, I'm 33. Now tell me what do you need? Why are you calling me? I'm in a hurry."

"All of you are always in a hurry. I was calling you for a reason. Umm, I cannot remember it now. You talk so much. And I forget."

"Ok tell me later when you can recall. I'm going to take my bag."

Anyhow her mother could recall immediately after Anu turned for the stairs.

"Give me a banana."

"Which banana? There is no banana now. I will bring while returning from the office. There are apples sliced on the table for you."

"Oh! You are always so busy that you even forget about the bananas your brother brought when he came home last week. They were bright yellow and big. Now for your carelessness, they are going to rot in freeze day after day." She grunted her dissatisfaction. Anu could not decide on her reaction.

Should she laugh or scream at her? This old woman sitting beside the window rutting on the bygone memory forgot everything. But bubbles of flashbacks floated on her mind sporadically though she lost track of time. Anu felt sorry for her though sometimes exasperation gripped her hectic daily struggles, and she wished to accuse her. "Why could not you love your daughter who was there always for you?" Anu felt cheated. Mother never loved her like her brother. But then she felt sad for this helpless woman. She had learned to forgive her long ago.

 How could she soothe this old woman who was detached from her son, her center of affection and cause of existence? Her son was everything to her. She could not bear the thought that her son needed her daughter-in-law's permission to visit her once a year. So, it was better to forget everything and live in peace than to remember and be in pain.

"It was not last week ma; it was a week one year ago when our Verodina blossomed in bright pink, and you fell very ill. Then he came to see you with bananas and stayed just for two hours following his wife's strict instruction."

But Anu could not say this to her. This would make her sad for some time until she forgets everything except the homecoming of her son last week and the bright, big bananas. Anu slipped out of the door instructing the ayah (caretaker) to take care of her. On her way back home, she would buy some bananas.

Come Back Somlata

No, no it is wrong. You cannot do this. You cannot make such a drastic decision. Come back Somlata. Come back.

Lata's show has stopped. Even the Santa Clause Auditorium has canceled her broadcast this evening.

"Somlata is under medical treatment due to fatal depression and nervous breakdown. She was rescued from her flat by her housekeeper after her suicide attempt three days ago." They have announced.

"Oh! Horrible! I cannot believe it." Everyone said.

No one believes it.

The most viewed, and most celebrated motivational speaker Somlata Sinha, tall, dark, beautiful with dark hair and a confident, cajoling smile is now lying inert under the daze of anesthesia. It is wrong.

Somlata means positivity, charisma, and simplicity. Somlata means there is no stress and no anxiety. Somlata means courage and indomitable energy.

Her voice ricocheted in every ear from morning to dawn. Her face flashed up at every corner of the city. She kindled a thousand hearts with her positive words and saved myriad lives from the dark abyss of frustration with her wise notes. She hosted the purpose of life. Her words flooded the channels, media, and auditoriums of different corners of the city. She announced the purpose of life, tore away the illusion of virtual life, and tried to show us self-worth.

But now 'Somlata' means a 'mystery.' Why did she take such a wrong step? How could such a positive soul think of self-destruction?

No one knows where she lives, what she does, whether she is married, and whether she has a child or not. You cannot assume her age from her face, as you never assumed her pain. Everything surrounding her was subdued, suppressed, and disguised.

Somlata has failed. It means we are defeated, every single soul who blindly follows her words, ideas, and beliefs.

But how can this be possible? She was so daunting a challenger of life! How could she yield to it? It cannot be. No, no, we do not believe it.

Gossip and rumors spread like wildfire. Somlata Sinha, a 32-year-old media sensation and motivational speaker, was married to a guy who had eloped with his new girlfriend. Somlata's only kid had died of thalassemia 5 years ago. And when after so long years she dares to love again, the man discards her with the accusation that she is very progressive-minded and does not suit an ideal wife. Meekness and docility must be ingrained in a perfect woman. And he realized that after two years of their relationship. For this validation of a nincompoop, Somlata is now fighting with life. How foolish! How wrong!

But it cannot justify everything. A girl like Somlata cannot give up her life for such triviality. It can be possible for us like Nasifa, Tinni, Manisha, Karan, and Minakshi, but for Somlata, it is impossible. All the strategies she propagandized, proved useless for herself, and now she is waiting for death. If she can fight others' fights, why can't she fight her own battle?

Come back Somlata. We are waiting for you. You cannot die this feather death, this death of a coward. Come back Somlata. Do not prove yourself false, whatever you have said, and we believed. Don't blow them as bubbles, mere words of a motivational speaker, prove their worth by coming back to us.

No One Killed Basabi

Basabi and I were school friends. Apart from other prospects, the same dark complexion and reticence of nature brought us close. I left Basabi after the intermediate as she went to the city for higher studies, and I remained in my old school in the village for the next two years. After that, we were admitted to two separate colleges. Communication gradually dwindled due to the pressure of study. More than that the real fact was no vacuum ever remains empty. Someone always remains there to take the new and the closest ones are most welcome.

In the hostel and college, I got acquainted with new friends and there remained little space to be sad for school days.

And then life started flying at a jet plane speed, career, marriage, children. Old faces got blurred and gradually memory erased them.

But the chance came suddenly one day. I got a message from one of my old friends over the phone to join a WhatsApp group. As I joined there amidst all the other school friends, I found Basabi. I saved the number. But before I could manage the time to call her, she called me.

And the gap of 15 years was waved away instantly within an hour. We talked as if we were never separated, old memories inundated our brains. Like two teenage girls, we went on sharing all the secrets we had accumulated in these years.

Old chord renewed and old friendship kindled with extra glory. On a Sunday morning, Basabi called me again. I was busy with household chores as it was the only day off at home when I had to arrange everything to start fresh on the hectic weekly schedule.

Her voice was weary and frustrated. I felt a nip in her voice like she had cried a lot. She shared her frustration. She was pregnant. But she thought she could not look after two children as she already had one and she nagged for miscarriage. She forced her husband to agree with her decision. But later she regretted her choice. She came to know it was a girl child and from then on, she started feeling vulnerable. Her mother blamed her for murdering a life. She took it in her heart and started lamenting over the lost embryo. Constant self-flagellation started chewing on her conscience.

I heard her patiently and advised her to forget everything. She had a lovely boy who was very brilliant and studious. I told her to love him more and keep herself engaged in productive work.

After that day we both became busy with our usual schedule of life. Sometimes we used to talk through messages. Sometimes she sent me her boy's home tasks that she could not solve. She even started a singing channel. She used to sing very sweetly. But again, another day she called me into my office and cried bitterly. She again started beating the dead horse when I was battling with tremendous work pressure. She said she could not forget, could not cope with her life, and could not concentrate on anything. Somewhere she was drifting away, tearing herself with her talon. The venom of depression engulfed her, and she started cussing herself. No way could I drag her from her self-built slammer.

Repeatedly, I tried to make her understand that she was spoiling her arranged life for something else that was not possible anymore. I suggested that she could take another baby. It might heal her wound.

But nothing works for her. She remained normal for some days but started behaving crazily again. Things got out of my hands when she contemplated suicide. I felt irritated. Life was an arduous struggle for me with the busy 24-hour schedule at home with my children, husband, and in-laws, and at the office. I had no time for those hypothetical sorrows. Gradually I stopped taking her calls or answering her messages on the excuse of work pressure.

She stopped calling me. Then one day I found her long painful message. She could not sleep because the bloody embryo was haunting her.

I shivered in irritation. Her call means monotonous depressing talks, and nagging despondency, which could not be healed. Whatever solution you referred to her she would not hear or follow. I even told her to consult a psychiatrist. But she never listened to me. She had enough time to wallow in sadness, but I had no time to hear the same record ad nauseum.

So, I just got busy with my life and shook away all her requests for a call as the tantrums of a spoiled baby.

One week passed and one day I was getting ready for a get-together party in my office in the evening.

As I was about to put my phone in my sling bag, I noticed a ping on the screen. I looked at it. An image was shared in our school WhatsApp group.

I didn't download it. I had no time. I slipped the phone into my bag and hurried towards the stairs.

I was late and tired when I came back. In the morning, I found continuous beeping on my mobile. I look at it in horror and tension. All the messages that popped up on the screen were shared by my school friends in the school group. The ground beneath me shattered and I felt tension building inside my heart.

With quivering fingers, I scrolled down the messages. I downloaded the images posted the previous night.

They were paper cutting, describing in brief, the unexpected suicide of a housewife at 48 Bidisha Sarkar Lane, Baharampur.

A thousand RIPs were flooding the screen.

No suicide notes were there to blame anybody and there was nobody to blame.

She was my best friend, once upon a time.

Why should I feel guilty? No one has killed Basabi after all.

Uproot

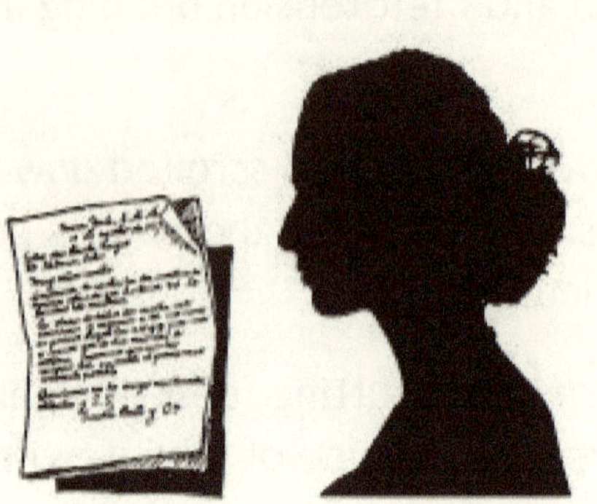

"Children, do you know the story of the foolish monkey who was appointed as a gardener?"

"Yes, Madam," They shout in chorus.

"Ok, then tell me. You, Trisha, tell me what happened to the saplings when the monkey took charge of taking care of them?"

"The monkey uprooted the trees before watering them. When the king came to visit his garden, he found all the trees dead. He asked the reason. The monkey admitted that he uprooted the trees to analyze how much water the trees needed."

"That's fine Trisha. Sit down."

The clock strikes five. The afternoon sun is peeping through the rusty bars like a shy bride. Its red robe, like a huge canopy shadows the dining hall where tiny heads scramble and make fun.

Sumita declares 'chuti' (termination of class) after checking their tasks. They scurry through the hallways and rush to the garden. She knows their habits. They will play there for some time before heading to their houses.

Sumita will miss them, terribly miss them.

But what should she do?

The letter is still there on her table, open and weighed down by an aqua-blue paperweight. Soumalya has written to her. He will come next month for some business issues in his previous company in Kolkata. He wishes to take her with him. He is her only son, her apple of eye.

Sumita did not respond at first. She never thought about it. Soumalya married on his wish. He just invited her to their ceremony along with other guests. She felt tremendously awkward when a person you knew so well suddenly changed so much that you could not recognize him. It seemed so abrupt, so undiscernible, and far beyond her contemplation. Sumita felt for the first time in her life the shore was receding beyond the horizon, and she was sure to fail to touch I, touch him, touch her son.

Soumalya only declared, "Mom I'm going to marry my classmate Sujata in university. You must come." No introduction, no invocation, no prelude, just formal informing. What scope was there for her to ask anything else?

The world consisted of only mother and son, and she never thought that one day she would be pushed to the brink of the cliff and be all alone.

But was that necessary? Sumita always tried to be his friend, best friend. She desperately put on two clothes of mother and father to be the whole, both part of the parents of her single child. Samiran died just two months after his birth.

She left no stone unturned to educate him, to support him, to raise him to a noble statute. And then one day he called her to invite her to his marriage ceremony. Sumita halted. She was so dumbfounded that even her breathing was not audible over the phone.

"Mom, are you there?"

"Yes."

"Have you any problem?"

"No, not at all."

"OK, I'll call you later and tell you in detail when to come and where. Bye now. Sujata's parents have come. There are a lot of things to settle, you know."

Something was boiling somewhere.

She had put the pulse to boil in the oven and forgot.

Oh my god! She hurried to the kitchen.

The burning smell was whirling within the four walls.

But she felt normal, as if it were normal, normal to get burnt, so easily.

The world was rotating around her, tossing the words, phrases, and information that she received just then.

And it was her last visit to her son. Sujata was the daughter of a rich businessman. They had bought a big house in Banaras. They had bought Soumalya also. Sumita felt embarrassed. How cheap he was!

She stayed only the night of the marriage ceremony when Sujata informed her, she would not come to the village. And Soumalya with a bowed down head just followed her to their bedroom. Sujata's parents shared some informal greetings and then ignored her. She could not adhere to the piteous looks of the guests and relatives and came back.

Questions after question, crooked comments tore her apart for these years. No one left to call her and sympathize.

"How are you, Sumita? How did these things happen? I cannot believe it when Bani Aunty calls me. How a boy like Soumalya could do this?"

Under their apparent sympathetic tone, exuberance was so raw that it pierced her like a poisoned arrow.

But gradually they stopped. One topic could not stir the same ripple for a long time. They started hunting for others' pain to gossip and relish.

Sumita also had changed in these years. Soumalya called her once or twice a month and most of the time from the office. Just some formal words and then hang up. His rich father-in-law had sent him to the U.S.A. for a degree. Soumalya promised to meet her before going to the U.S.A. But he could not keep the promise.

Sumita used to work in a school. After retirement, she started gardening and tutoring the local children. She had also planned to start an online course on Easy Mathematics Tips. She loved to solve tricky puzzles, though she could not solve the puzzle of her own life.

Every burn gets healed but leaves a scar. She tried to live again on her own but those struggles of long years were not so easy to forget.

This winter the garden is blooming with numerous flowers, and she arranged a picnic with her students. It was a source of boundless joy. And the people were accommodating. Though urban air is sweeping out the rural smells fast, this part is not yet so affected. Life is serene and simple here.

Sumita is getting old, and the complexities of old age are gnawing now and then along with fear and insecurity. But she has learned to accept it. All her life she fought alone for her son. Now she must live, live for her own.

But the letter is sprawling over there like a brazen shock. She starts rereading it. They have a kid, and they are returning to settle in Banaras. Sujata must join her office as the maternity leave is finished and they need a housekeeper, and a faithful caretaker for their baby. Sujata's parents have a serious business. So, they cannot be permanent. Soumalya will come to take Sumita and this time he proves his maturity by asking her permission.

This is her life, and she must make the decision.

The children are shouting, "Madam, madam."

"What happened?"

She rises from her trance and rushes out holding the letter in her hand.

"Helicopter, there is a helicopter," They cry excitedly indicating their hands to the sky where a giant black grasshopper is circling making mechanical buzzes. Sumita tries to look at the sky adjusting her glasses over the nose.

"Where, where?"

Suddenly a gust of truant wind sweeps away the letter from her hand. Like an airplane, it takes wings and glides in high air.

Sumita does not try to catch it. The children run after it.

"Let it go." She will tell Soumalya her decision. A smile of peace permeates her face. She will never allow any foolish monkey in her garden to uproot her peace. In the encroaching evening, she enters the house and waits for dawn. Some petunia will bloom tomorrow.

Long-forgotten Line

The sunlight is profusing liberally through the ungrudging bars of the rusty, oxidized window. Mithila stares with her old opaque eyes at the brazen dazzling spikes on her open book, "The Book Thief" by Markus Zusak, worn out after several rereadings. It stirs her memory to something, or someone, blurry but tangible. Her heart pounds in a desperate attempt to recall the name, so intricately carved in her soul.

She closes her eyes and opens- a face, not a face, but a part of it, twist of lips, arrogantly amusing in a controlled smile, from the bush of dense beard and mustache and the eyes searching deep, hit her tarnished memory. "That's it"- she exclaims, like a child at the success of recalling the long-forgotten lines of rhyme. That smile matches the sunlight, spreading over beautifully like an ancient symbol of excavated civilization, magical and mystic.

It was a long time, three decades, and more. Now Mithila is sixty-five and all alone. Nitesh, her husband died five years ago. Mainak, and Manisha, her son, and daughter, are happily settled in their cities, in their own families. They call her once or twice a week, and that she feels enough for an old woman, waiting for death, in the custody of a belligerent housekeeper.

She met him on her blog, "Drafts of Sadness." He was an avid reader of her poetry and a confidante in her attempt to explore the riddle of the literary labyrinth. And she could not think back how he broke the ice of detached aloofness, and the cloak of self-abrogation from her, with his exclusive patience and simplicity of behavior. He made her feel the emotions, the intonation of love, written in the pages of books, and in real life intertwining them in a magic piquancy. She never propped to his appropriateness, but she felt what he just wanted her to feel or pretended to be.

"I love you without knowing how, or when, or from where.

I love you straightforwardly, without complexities or pride.

So, I love you because I know no other way than this: where I do not exist, nor you,

*So close that your hand on my chest is my hand, so close that your eyes close as I fall asleep." (**XVII I Do not Love You** by **Pablo Neruda**)*

*"I want to do with you what spring does with the cherry trees."(**Every Day You Play** by* **Pablo Neruda)**

He used to quote Pablo Neruda with all its sultry sensuality, and poetic emblem, wafting her like a feather, lost and light. Her songs, her slices of solitude got intoned in his assurances, in his longing for her company- "I love to talk to you; I feel comfortable with you; I like you so much." Oh! How these words ramble through her trafficked memory even now, twitching her lips into a suppressed smile!

He was so eager to know what she was doing, what she was reading, why she was sniffing, whether she was taking medicine or not, and he wanted to see her desperately.

Everything was fine till the day she disclosed the truth just casually, "My husband is at home today, so we will talk tomorrow. Just keep on reading "The Book Thief." You may feel a little bored at first, but it will be worth it later." At that moment she could not apprehend his flinching back in shock or disappointment through the safety sojourn of virtual media where only his voice could be heard. But very soon she felt the flakes of frosty formality in him, burying the warmth of their relationship. And the detachment of his behavior was more deadly than anything else in her life.

She took him as one who could be with her just as she wished him to be as her book lover, her soul mate, unblemished from any earthly atrocity, purely eternal. But she never thought that her heart would be at stake in this way, in a constant fire, in piercing pain, and insatiable desires. His words, and songs, so simple, so earthly, so loving and caring like old books, yellowish and smelling of affection, kept haunting her, slashing her in deep bruises. A single simple message from him could do the magic, could wash away all the anger, and hurt heaped in her weak rib bone, just a "hi" or "how are you" Or "which book you are reading now?" Yes, the last one would be the best. But nothing happened. She just waited and waited in perturbed silence to watch him vanish.

Her husband started accusing her of her absentmindedness, her son's homework got neglected, her in-law's medicines skipped, and she waned away. What could she do? She was prepared for his departure any day, any time, but not like this. It could be a great leave-taking proclaiming mutual love, and respect and with the promise to keep the memory in the hearts, not in this frantic abrupt way mitigating all those dreams they piled together in debris and mutilating her in a dead body. There was no need to prove her wrong in that way.

After one month when she erased him from the screen memory, she felt "it is the time to kill him" from her brain-ROM. She started drafting her story, the story of a virtual love that got betrayed and assaulted. She poured her anguished heart into her pen and smeared it with ink. It took a week to finish and edit it, giving it perfect shape. She was happy at her creation, a beautiful short story ready to be published in her blog from where it was once born. And in her heart, she felt he was buried. Her hatred, her abhorrence, and her self-pity murdered her blind emotions at last.

 But then why did the sunlight remind her of him after long years?

The Kitten and Cleopatra

I open the door; a cold heartless breeze hits my face. I inhale sharply and my nose flares in the singeing dryness and my fatigued legs follow the night mist beyond the balcony touching the cement bars that decorate it in a semicircle fixture. I check out but there is not a single house lit in this wintry haze except the mist-coated streetlights and occasional flashing of headlights. Who dares to touch the death from the warmth of a quilt?

Only I.

Tonight.

Now.

I hadn't slept for the past ten days, tossing, and turning in my cozy little bed as if it were ablaze, consumed by the fury burning inside me.

The deep, dark agony of loss and despair wreaked havoc in my heart. And now this frigid wind has nothing to do with my frail body as my soul is in the fire.

Everything is fair in love and war. But it is not fair when a man makes a woman fall in love with all the loveliest pleasures and persuasions and then abruptly tears apart the bond keeping her in mid-stream to get washed away in grief.

He loved me more than I loved him. He cared for me more than I could. He entrusted within me the elixir of love, care, concern, passion, everything. He made me laugh with his humor and uplifted me from my poor existence to a living panorama of color and loveliness. All the support and concern he offered helped me to fight back in my life. He kept me busy with his continuous indulgence and childishness. I felt important. I was the queen of his kingdom.

But now he is gone. I cannot contact him, I get no messages, and no phone calls. I thought he might be busy. I waited for him to be free. I waited, waited, and waited. Then I got irritated. I lost my patience. He did not answer my call. Even when he answered, his voice remained curt and crispy as if he were not interested in starting the conversation. He, who kept my inbox filled with thousands of messages, did not even answer my billions. My every pleading, every accusation, my torment, my cry just made him more aloof, more obnoxious, more indifferent. I accused him of cruelty - he treated me more cruelly. I lay vacant day after day. In the daytime, I dragged my body to the office, made every mistake, and waited to be snapped. I tried my best to keep myself busy, not to think over it, and not to check my phone repeatedly but I could not help it. The question kept me haunted, "Why did he do so? He loved me. How could he hurt me, neglect me, keep me in pain and agony?" Every day I used to wake up to his call, his loving words. Every day I worked with a happy heart with his continuous interruption. His over-pampering concern and indulging affection kept my butterfly heart always in flapping mode. It was so peaceful, so heavenly. He did not even allow me to sleep at night. If I fell asleep, he called me and woke me up. I had to chat with him till dawn broke upon my windowpane and morning mist dribbled across it. I protested and reasoned to have sound sleep at night as it was an unhealthy habit, and it would spoil my health. But he did not pay heed to my words. He teased me as a 'good girl' who lived by the rules. So, I broke all the rules for him. I learned to love crazily and to fly with it. I dissolved my soul, my body within him. I lived in his wish, in his pleasure, in his way. I remained for him for every single breath of my life. I lived for him- a life that he had given me, colored by his wish, desire and that symphonizes with mine. I liked it. I loved it. I liked to live with him every moment. Then everything changed within one month. One month = 30 days(approximately) = (30*24) hours= {30*(24*60)} minutes. So, there was a lot of time, hours, minutes, seconds, and much more, a long time to get transformed from pupa to butterfly. And I changed a lot. My lonely, frail, rigid, indifferent soul stooped in total worship to be his. Then why?

I was crazy to pull out the answer. I texted him, and called him, asking the reason. He never asked me to break the relationship or accused me of any drawbacks. But he stayed calm, cool, and aloof in front of all my sobbing queries, and blaming. He just cast himself more forlorn, more detached, as I wanted to touch him, to know the cause. "Why did he stop loving me?" "What have I done to him?" The questions kept haunting me even in my sleep. When my puzzled heart snapped him with a hundred 'whys' he just answered, "Sleep well, good night."

I searched for the reason and dug it within me. My life without him was not colorful, but it was not so vulnerable. I could take my food and could sleep my hours in solitude. If you call it peaceful then it was so. I wanted to go back to that life. But the distance is now too much, and one cannot back walk long distances. I am not a crab. I realized he was no longer there for me. He no longer needed me. He could not cut me off, but he could not love me anyhow. Sometimes he called me, just for one or two seconds. I could not force him, could not remind him repeatedly how he loved me once and how miserable he had left me. I found no sleep, no solace in anything. My eyes burned in agony, not a drop of water was left to wet the eyelashes. I was dying of thirst and fever.

So, I decided to die. My life is a heavy burden for me that I want to get rid of. I accuse no one. There will be no single scrap of paper that can be found in my room as proof of my unnatural death. A melancholy melody was playing somewhere, maybe a song from the '70s. I do not like to sing or hear songs anymore. It just makes me disturbed and restless. It dishevels my heart in bitter tears and makes me mad. One day I loved songs. He used to send me a song every day. And I used to hear that repeatedly. I used to feel him within the song. I hummed it all day long and the next day till the new song beeped on my screen, Adele or Avril or Colbie Caillat, Ben Howard's 'Only Love', Westlife's 'I Wanna Grow Old with You', Christina Perri's 'A Thousand Years' and Ellie Goulding's 'Love me like you do'. I was crazy for them. Then gradually it became less and less and finally stopped totally. I waited and hummed the same song for three days, then for four days, five days, seven days and then I got irritated to sing any song. My boss called me thrice and I did not respond. I knew I had lost my job. I cared a fig. I cared for nothing.

And there is none to care for me. After I die, my "Little Heaven" the orphanage home, where I was brought up, will be contacted and they will, celebrate an extra Black Day when every day is black for them. I sigh and touch the hazy mist with my cold finger. Getting a house for rent in this low-cost suburban area is not easy and there is so much demand. If I die today, a new tenant will be the next day. Nothing will be disturbed or interrupted without me. I can die without any acquisition at this time, when everything is so calm and cool, and the world is so peaceful. I step forward to the brim of the balcony and peep below. Freezing wind shivers my blood.

"Mew"

The mew of a kitten. I bend more, except a few more to touch death and I see him in the streetlight. A snow-white furry ball, muddled in blood, is laying curled in the road and a little kitten is poking her, crying bitterly – "mew, mew."

I forget everything. I calculate the situation-the mother has died in an accident and the little one is trying to awaken the dead. I tried this twenty years ago. The car-crushed body of my mom flashed in front of me and the face of one who snatched me from death. I was jerking her blindly to wake her up from the pool of blood. Suddenly one person yanked my hand and lifted me in his lap before a lorry could squash me on the road. Oh, God! I rushed downstairs. My weak, starved body, suffering soul, gathers all the strength to run down those stairs and to reach the street where I find him, whimpering. I pick him up against the queue of rushing cars. He looks at me astonishingly and says 'Mew.' We come back. I clean him. Then we drink warm chocolate milk and cookies together. I put him on my bed beside me with an old towel and covered both of us with a blanket. I feel sleepy and it is a cold January night in Mumbai.

I fell in love again.

Lullaby

(The old song)

"Ma you are humming the song that you used to sing when I was a baby in your lap. I could recall the whole note from then."

"Yeah, it's that song. But you cannot remember it as the cradled baby. I sang the whole song that night at our home party when you reached your golden five years. Then you may have learned it."

"No, no, it's not the fact. Even that night when you startled everyone with that lullaby, enthralling and pensive with a vibrant trill, no one noticed that I was there to chorus with you. I knew the hymn ma, from the ancient hours of my birth."

"How is it possible?"

"You are laughing. You are mocking me, ma. But it's true. The song was ingrained in my memory when I was inside you, in the cozy warmth of your womb. Who is the singer of that song ma, that soothing, emolument song?"

"I don't know. I heard my mother singing this at the time of my childhood and she might be at her time with her ma, my grandma. It's a case of transmission from generation to generation like the ancient "Vedas.""

 "But I have decided that I'll not sing it to my children. What should she or he get out of it? What have I got - the flooding emotion and no practicality, as Sushant always accused me of. He wished that our children would not be like me, impulsive, emotional, and frail but like him- practical, bold, smart. I must prepare a new lullaby that will speak of this world, this society, and this traumatic existence of us.

Lullaby

 (The new song)

"Mom, you are still awake! Oh, Mom, I told you several times, not to wait for me, just put my food on the table and sleep comfortably."

"How can a mother sleep comfortably when her daughter has not returned even at this odd hour of the night, how can I?"

"Mom, you are childish, I am fading up with you. Why do not you understand, I'm a grown-up lady, no more your little cheek."

"You all are grown-ups and know everything. But whatever it is, for my part, it is impossible to close my eyes in peace when my blood is out in the dark, cold, night. May I ask you what kept you engaged till this time outside?"

"Come on Mom, cool down. It is you who taught me from my childhood to fight against wrongs; it is you who showed me the vulnerable world where only powerful politicians held the vantage point of every opportunity and affluence in life. It is you Mom, who led me this way, where under every mask there hid an animal, under every smile a bloodthirsty soul. Those are your lullabies for me, Mom. And now I'm in that vocation to strip off the disguise of a smoothly woven plot and highlight the truth in my column, in my journal. Thousands of hands will pick them tomorrow morning with the crowing of roosters and clinking of cycles when the paper men throw them to their veranda. Thousands will click their news app to know the truth. Do you realize that, Mom? I must finish the news that I set up day by day, bit by bit, a heinous trap that is hatched under our noses and coated with the smell of chocolate and vanilla. That industry that makes cookies also makes something else Mom. And I know what it is."

"Oh! But I'm scared. Oh, baby, what have I done to you? You are at risk, for me. I have diverted your blossoming young heart to this social restlessness. It is me, who instead of chanting the song of nature, and love, sang the song of rebellion. I discarded my mother's lullaby and sang the new songs of a practical world. Oh, how horrible I am!"

"No Mom, you are not. What have you gained being the listener of that lullaby that you heard in your childhood and that you regret not injecting into me? What have you got

Mom? Father rejected you for a smart lady who can sing Beetles and Bob Morley. And you remain as an epitome of failure even in the eyes of your parents, but not to me Mom. To me, you are the strength, the flame that flickers under the black cloak of clouds. You are a great creator of lullabies."

"Do you remember the songs?"

"The songs, I remember those all, 'His name was John Henry', 'Come on the road, and you will know your destination', and that 'blood simmering song', you called it, 'Who has broken my home, I can recall them, my days sowed in blood, hammering in my conscience', and the innumerable songs you used to sing mom. They were so overwhelming and electrifying for me. I cannot make you understand how I felt when you sang them with all your spirit when you and I were there only, and no one. Papa's office tour was then so frequent and lengthy, but it did not affect your voice. Maybe I was wrong. Your songs were your showoff, your desperate attempt to conceal the gnawing pain. But if it was so, then why do you stop Mom? Nowadays, you just keep nagging at me.

Why are you so afraid, afraid of what Mom? What is left for us to lose?"

"Nothing, nothing, except the trauma if you don't come back to me if anything wrong happens to you. How can I live then? Sushant has left me. And now you are my only abode, only reason to live."

"You have to learn to live on your own, for your own happiness. In this world, we are mere pawns, fighting fruitless fights. Now come on, serve me the food, and then we will sleep together. You must sing the songs - your lullabies in my sleep."

Mad Woman in the Attic

"Cannot you love me a bit and talk to me? I am getting old and ill. I will die very soon." Mridula whispered to her husband in a pleading tone.

"What should I say?" His cold voice chilled her blood as if an ice blade had torn the heart apart. In his dark face, there was not a single ray of love or sympathy, even a trace of pity.

She gasped for breath. Her hazy eyes observed the steps he took to mound the stairs leading to his room. His room, his house, his life, his decision. How easy it was for him to live the life he chose!

Sometimes he would look at her, not particularly at her face but at something behind or beside her. She was always invisible to him.

She could not remember the last time she lived her life. She could only remember her childhood days and the days at her school, and her home. Where was her home? They said after marriage a woman's home is with her husband. But was this her home?

She tried to scoop for some happy memories, memories of love and feelings. But she did not find that face she wished to be happy with.

How much did she get him? He was so busy with his relatives, relatives' relatives, and students, and there were so many things in his life, his life where she never found her own. She was never there, never, in his life. She was in the kitchen, in the bed, in the laundry, in the garden- cleaning, making food, serving, and washing. She was there- bearing children, caring, and rearing them up. She was there to fulfill others' dreams. What was her own?

It was a long time since he took her to the doctor. They did not believe her, her husband, and the children. Something was gnawing at her brain, and someone was talking incessantly. They laughed, taunted, threw furtive glances, and tried to make her understand that she was making things in her silly little head. Whenever she closed her eyes, memories haunted her, memories of loveless days, as if she were drilling and drifting under the voices, familiar but cold.

Sometimes she went on laughing, laughing for hours and then she started crying. Medicine could not do any miracle. There was no hand on her shoulder or no voice to soothe her. They were busy. Busy, busy, busy, always.

The food started burning, the clothes got burnt under the iron heat, the garden remained untilled, and the house was in disarray. People started talking. Everyone knew she was mad, a mad woman in the house. There was no attic and there was no cook or housekeeper. She could take her exile into the room where the yellow wallpaper could peel her sorrows off the wall.

"Love me, talk to me" she whispered. The wind heard her, the searing asphalt road, the dazzling sun, stormy eyes of a nimbus cloud listened to her. But he did not. She heard his voice over the phone, narrating her insanity to everyone he knew or did not know. He was narrating his pathetic life being the husband of such a woman.

He was talking, laughing, and gossiping with everyone but not with her.

She demanded, "Talk to me."

'What should I talk about with you, Mridula?'

"About everything, the books you are writing, the people you are meeting, the life you are living. About the weather, sudden heat surge in Mid-Asian countries, declaration of wars, Putin's new policies, or the wife of Barack Obama. Anything you will talk about, I'm here to listen."

"I've no time. I'm busy."

He brushed her aside and shut himself in her study. He remained there till noon, night, early morning, except for eating or taking a bath or some jobs of his own. He ate and talked over the phone. He wrote and got tired of writing and talked over the phone for hours, he talked garrulously, narrating the same story repeatedly, the story of his life, so hard with a mad woman, and his success story of becoming a writer even in the face of such adversity.

He was great, so great! Didn't they understand?

"Give me medicine. More medicine. I need to sleep. Someone talks within me, eating away at my sanity and driving me to madness. I want to stop them. Ominous words, burning words."

And she slept for hours after hours as if she wished to forget everything. She did not want to open her eyes and visit the world. It was so suffocating here, no air, no love. It was better to sleep, goddess of oblivion. She did not want to remember if there was something like an eraser that could erase her memories forever.

No one will wait for her to wake. And if she slept forever no one would be there to wake.

They would come and console her husband, "How you had to live and struggle and to do such great jobs!"

Then they must look at her sleeping body, whimpering in her dream, "Love me, love me, talk with me."

They stopped facing her and started behaving more viciously. Their stern looks piercing. Her blood chilled. They talked and talked more over the phone. Even their whispers were earsplitting.

She tried to sleep, one, two, or three pills at a time.

There they applauded his success. This year he published four books on the lives of generous women in India. They sold well. He narrated their sufferings and struggles, their oppression and humiliation in society, and the family. People talked about his books. The house was crowded with photographers and publishers.

His smiling face was on the paper, on the dazzling screen. She looked and could not recognize him. He could smile and talk.

They discarded her. They did not look at her anymore as if she were invisible. They talked among themselves, discussed, and laughed.

"I'm here, I'm here." She whispered.

They pretended to be blind. They could not see her, waiting eagerly for their attention.

One, two, three, four, five, six, she turned over the bottle on her skinny palm and swallowed. The gulping noise mixed with the noise of the watch- tik, tok, tik, tok.

He was absent from the house. There was a ceremony to attend. She heard him talking over the phone. He had been nominated the best writer of the year for his writings on the lives of women. She tiptoed into his room. He had gone to receive his prize. Only the smell of his cologne was wafting in her trespassing sighs.

There were the books, stacked perfectly behind the glass chamber. She took one after another and looked at the pages. Something broiled within her, a tingling sensation, peeled with laughter. She started laughing. As she flipped the pages her laughter increased. What a hypocrisy! The women in the pages of books looked at her. They looked hurt.

"Go away mad woman, don't scare us, don't taint our glory with your dirty fingers. Go to sleep "

"I'll."

She stacked all the books around her and made a bed - a pyre. Then she sparked matchsticks one after another and threw them on them.

"Go to sleep, go to sleep," The women of the book screamed out.

"You, mad woman, go to sleep." They howled repeatedly from the leaping fire.

The books started burning. She smelt the burnt paper and smiled peacefully.

Now she could sleep.

She exclaimed, "Come women, let's all sleep together. You and me. We all are mad women in this attic, room, and world."

The Shut Door

The letter is lying passive on the table under the forgotten apple of Eve. And my heart is etherized not in the same inertness but in agonizing pain, enough to numb my senses. The pain that I never felt so intense before, puzzles me now. It happens sometimes you cannot recognize yourself.

Sitesh has died. My husband has died last week. They have contacted me at my office address. And it took seven days to reach the news of a man who is now unreachable. There was no other way of communication. I left none for him, for anyone. It was my self-declared exile.

Death was inevitable for every mortal. So why do I care? Let him die in his stubborn way. He never listened to me. Never. He never cared for my emotions. Never. Why should I cry for his death? It was as easy and natural as my pet cat. Despite my continuous persuasion, it entered the warm mud oven on a chilly night, secretly, and could not escape when in the morning I flamed it to cook food. But when I found its scorched body, I cried, cried bitterly, and blamed myself for not closing the kitchen door the previous night.

But for Sitesh nothing to blame. In his death, he reached his salvation.

We were separated for ten long years. At the age of forty-five, there was no need to go for legal procedure. And Sitesh also had no such vibe to face the scornful jeer of the world. I demanded and he agreed with silent approbation. That was our mutual negotiation and that was enough. I had done my duties. Our only son is well settled with twin girls and a good life partner. Sometimes he visited me, sometimes he went to Sitesh. I think so, though he never confessed his visit to his father to me. But children are innocent. They cannot lie or hide. I don't blame Ritesh, my son. We all like to live behind that curtain of cozy lies. What we see or feel, we often hide its impact from others. We don't even want to acknowledge that we are aware of it.

I couldn't continue the relationship. I lived my blooming years in the caged murky sky of

Crasher Station. All the area was full of dust of stone chips, vulgar abusive words of workers as their spit of betel leaf, and the frivolous giggling of young girls. Ritesh was sent to a hostel after he completed his High School. This vicious unhealthy environment didn't affect him. He was raised under the cultured pruning of sophistication. But I had to wait, wait for Ritesh to grow up and get settled. Then I would be free. I had no job. But when Ritesh started for his job exams, I also started mine. And finally, I cracked one.

The posting was far from Siamanpur, the world where only stones are chipped, and dust are inhaled. I wanted to flee far from that barren dusty world. It was a private farm. No big salary, no big security. But enough for my livelihood. When I told Sitesh my final decision, he just looked at me for a long time. Then with an uneasy perturbation and defeat in those eyes, he dashed out from the room. He knew I hated the atmosphere of Siamanpur and his intimacy with the working girls. Many a night he didn't come back home on the pretext of superintending the supply trucks. But he couldn't hide from me the smell of stinking hooch and sweat of those girls.

I never said anything. At first, I separated my room and bed and then my life from him.

On the day of my departure, Sitesh looked at me. Some pain was there, some pleading. I asked him to go with me. Yes, there was urgency, honesty, and a wish to get him out of this hell. But he denied it. I rode away through the gravel path on the rickshaw on a misty dawn of January. He went back on his trodden path. Before taking the last turn, I looked at him. His stubborn shoulders were stooped, and his head hung low. Fresh dew was glistening on his rough, disheveled hair. I wished to go and drag him away with me.

But I never showed that force. I just silently went away, far away from him, so far away from where returning was just impossible. I never want to reach the bedrock of his emotions and never let him reach mine. We just drift apart.

Am I blaming myself? Am I sad? I was not responsible for the cat dying, but I forgot to latch the kitchen door. For Sitesh I shut the door and did not let him enter.

Written in Blood

Asima was lying half-conscious on the floor.

Blood streaming from her left jaw marked a deep red on the worn-out floor. The battle had finished in the evening. And the hut was cloaked in uncanny silence. Her cheek was stinging where he had smacked hard.

Her three daughters were standing, huddling beside the string cot at the corner of the room, watching and whispering to each other. Her son had not returned home like most of the days. It was fine not to return. Where was the place to give a grown-up boy to sleep in this little two-room cottage? In the adjoining room, the utensils, and sacks of grains with poultry food were stacked together leaving not a single place for footfall.

Ratan usually spent the night at a certain corner of the wine shop. Lately, however, he had been coming home early and spending the nights behaving quite decently. He had even gone as far as to dye his graying hair, enough to arouse suspicion.

Suddenly, Ratan rushed into the room and splashed something over her. Tremendous burning pain revived her consciousness. She screamed and screamed. Three daughters started wailing. A heavy black curtain fell on her.

When she woke up, she found herself in the corridor of a hospital. The bed is never available for common people. Saline water was dripping through the tube pushing her shriveled veins to panic. Buzzing flies were swarming on her wounds. She tried to raise her body. But piercing pain pinned her in that dirty molded bed. A tremendous thirst parched her throat. She tried to call out for water, but only a hoarse, muted rasp escaped her scorched throat. It could not reach any sympathetic ear above the din of the hospital corridor.

She had given birth to six children one after another. Five daughters and finally a boy. Ratan was furious but couldn't throw her out of the house for giving birth to so many daughters. She was grateful to him for that reason. But how could he do this at this age when the children were all grown up and the house was full of grandchildren? Five daughters got married and they gave birth to children. For every birth, Asima had to stay with them for months. What could she do?

Ratan accused her of not giving him company in bed. And that he claimed as his reason for sleeping with other women. When one-night Asima discovered Ratan with another woman, she was shocked. She yelled at Ratan and hurled utensils at the unknown woman. Ratan got furious. He accused her of being a useless wife and beat her mercilessly. Asima couldn't protest. She was amputated with agony and the pain of betrayal. It was not the first time. He would beat her occasionally under the daze of alcohol. To make ends meet she had to work hard on others' families. Ratan could not work. Excessive wine had damaged his liver. He was weak. But how could he gather such power when he used it to beat Asima? Could she not counterattack? She could. She had more strength than him. But conventional society never teaches a woman to strike back. The seed of morality was shown so deep in her heart. But this time he threw acid on her.

He had damaged her to the extreme. Amidst the buzzing flies on her wounds, she contemplated what she should do.

Two months had passed in that dingy dirty corridor. Asima had healed a bit physically. But the wound raking inside her sent waves of pain, periodically driving her into a frenzy.

She had lost all hope. In these two months, no one had come from her home, not even her children. They had left her to die like a discarded old pet. Only the police came for some inquiry. They did not seem so interested, just routine work. Family brawling is quite common though throwing acid is a severe crime. But Asima told them it was her mistake. She mistook it as plain water and splashed it on her face. It was an unbelievable story, but the police believed her as she behaved stubbornly on her account. Inside her heart, she felt Ratan would come to visit her, hold her hands, ask forgiveness, and take her home. But as days passed by the hope started to fade. Amidst the crowded corridor, not a familiar face was seen. Even her children had discarded her for whom she toiled dawn to dusk. Asima pondered on. Doctors had prescribed some tests that were not free in the hospital and some emergency medicines were needed. The phone was not available. So, they have nothing more to do except kick her out of the meager place that she had been occupied for days. Their indifferent, pitiful eyes were turning into hateful glare. Reality gradually took root in Asima's heart. They had discarded her like a tattered cloth. She would no longer be of any use to them.

"Go away you wretched woman, show your burnt face somewhere else." They want to say.

Asima looked at the deluge of people swarming all over. It was the visiting hour. Nothing would happen if she joined the crowd. The scars on her face had made her easily recognizable. But people no longer care about unnecessary troubles.

Asima hid her face with the fringe of her dirty saree. She was not afraid of people, but people might get afraid of her. When she stepped on the footpath leaving the iron gate of the hospital behind, darkness engulfed the surroundings. People were rushing to reach their destination to avoid the blow of a heavy torrent. Where would Asima go? She waited under a shed. A dog was coiling before her. The sky seemed merciless.

Rainwater was flooding the roads. Her clothes were soddening with the splash of delinquent drops and mud. Asima stepped on the pavement. The gushing water hissed above her ankle. Heavy rain pelted upon her. Asima did not try to hunch her shoulders against the merciless downpour. She let the cold-water wash over her jagged face. For the first time in her life, someone touched her so lovingly.

Blooming moonlight reflecting on the water glistened like a silver light of hope. Asima dipped her toes in the water and the silver shafts broke into a thousand ripples. Where would she find her hope now?

Who is the author?

If Betty Smith can say, "the world was hers for the reading," then obviously it is true for someone whose passion takes the first sip of a book to read and relish. As an introvert in nature, Munmun Samanta (Sam) always finds her secret shade amidst the smell of books and loves to scribble her thoughts in ink and paper. Born in West Bengal, India, by profession she is a teacher of English. Her career as a writer started with college and university magazines and later, she rejoined as a Blogger.

She started writing on her page: Yellow Chrysanthemum and on her blogs: samslibrary.com and phoenixfabulist. In. Her works have been published in various literary magazines and anthologies: "Bridge," published in November 2020 by Eric Publication celebrates the poets of East and West; "Immortal Inkings'" published by Papermint Books publication captures some of her multilayered thoughts in the framework of poetic invasion. In this anthology "Cosmic Rainbow" by Eric Publication, she contributed ten poems, all of which are entirely individual in approach and impulse like the distinct colors of a Rainbow. But her prior love is navigated in her short stories. Sweetycat Press, a US-based publishing house, published her short stories. And here in this short anthology, "Yellow Chrysanthemum," she has compiled twenty of her stories that capture the multilayered psychic journey of twenty women, discriminated against and devitalized in every respect by social bigotry. Writing, for her, is not a skill but a source of power, shelter from the vicious onslaught of everyday life. She believes in the magic of words more than anything else. Every story she knitted is a slice of her soul bricked and plastered by her raw emotion. Author Contact: munu.ruku2020@gmail.com

Facebook Page:
https://www.facebook.com/immortalinkling/

Book Review blog: https://samslibrary.com/

Story Blog:

https://phoenixfabulist.in/

Instagram:

https://www.instagram.com/munu.ruku/

YouTube Channel:
https://www.youtube.com/channel/UCFLCC4
_2JujnryV9veFsW1

Facebook:

https://www.facebook.com/munu.ruku

LinkedIn:

https://www.linkedin.com/in/munmun-rudra-734136212/

Goodreads:
https://www.goodreads.com/bookwormsreview

Twitter:

https://twitter.com/Munuruku

 Medium.com
https://medium.com/@munu.ruku2020

Acknowledgments

I am grateful to the countless women whose lives and experiences inspired this unified voice.
Thanks to these literary magazines for publishing the literary pieces included in this book.

"Caged Bird Sings Another Song" *You Are the Poem (2021)*

"Long Forgotten Lines" *Bubble (2021, Vol-1)*

"Mother India" *Fine Lines (Summer, 2024)*

Thank you to the early reviewers.

Thank you to Jill Sharon Kimmelman for writing the Foreword.

Thank you to Aaron Burden for contributing his beautiful Cover Photograph
AaronBurden.com